This book belongs to

For Jack and Herbert

G.B.

This edition published by Parragon Books Ltd in 2013 and distributed by

Parragon Inc.
440 Park Avenue South, 13th Floor
New York, NY 10016
www.parragon.com

Published by arrangement with Gullane Children's Books

Text and illustrations © Georgie Birkett 2013

ISBN 978-1-4723-3183-0

Printed in China

Hogbert's Spring

Georgie Birkett

PaRRagon

Bath · New York · Singapore · Hong Kong · Cologne · Delhi
Melbourne · Amsterdam · Johannesburg · Shenzhen

In the Bramble House, Hogbert and his family were just waking up from a long winter's sleep. "Spring is coming!" smiled Mommyhog, as she stretched and yawned. "What's Spring?" wondered Hogbert, and he stepped outside to look for it.

In the sky, the sun shone brightly.
Hogbert looked up and saw a nest
and a feathery creature with a pointed mouth.

"Are you Spring?"
Hogbert asked.

"I am a very busy bird, my dear.
I'm keeping these eggs warm.
But Spring is on its way."

Sitting on a leaf was a bright, stripy, wiggly thing.

"Are you Spring?" asked Hogbert.

"I am a hairy caterpillar.
But Spring isn't far away,"
it said.

All of a sudden, a warm raindrop bounced off of
Hogbert's nose.
In the sky above him was a rain cloud.
Lying in the wet grass was another cloud.

"Are you Spring?" asked Hogbert.

"Baa baa," replied the cloud . . .

. . . and trotted away on four short legs!

Hogbert rested in the grass.
Shoots grew up around his toes.
A ladybug landed on his nose.

Hogbert was wondering where to look next,
when he heard bouncy footsteps....

Up popped a furry thing with a bushy tail,
jumping up and down with excitement!

"You must be Spring!" cried Hogbert.

"No, I'm Jeremy!"
he laughed.
"Do you want to play?"

Playing was so much fun that Hogbert forgot all about Spring.
He didn't notice the leaves on the trees unfolding
or the flower buds stretching up to the sky.

Eventually, Mommyhog called from the Bramble House.
"Goodbye, Jeremy," said Hogbert.
"See you soon!"

Hogbert's brothers and sisters were very excited.
"Spring has arrived!" they cried.
"Quick, get ready! Polish your nose!"
"Are you sure?" said Hogbert. "Spring wasn't there when I looked!"

Mommyhog smiled and led them out into the yard.
"Look very closely, Hogbert!" she said.

"Where are your eggs?"
Hogbert asked the busy bird.

"I don't have eggs anymore,
my dear, but five
chirping chicks!"

"What about the
caterpillar?" said Hogbert.

"I'm not a caterpillar
anymore, I'm a
butterfly!" it cried.

"And the big white cloud?" asked Hogbert.

"It wasn't a cloud," said Mommyhog,
"it was a sheep—and now she has three
leaping lambs."

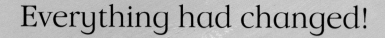

Everything had changed!

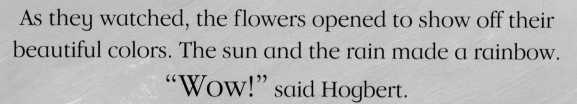

As they watched, the flowers opened to show off their beautiful colors. The sun and the rain made a rainbow.
"WOW!" said Hogbert.

Then he heard bouncy footsteps.
Hogbert wondered if Jeremy had changed, too?

But no—Jeremy was just the same!
"Come on, Hogbert, let's play!"